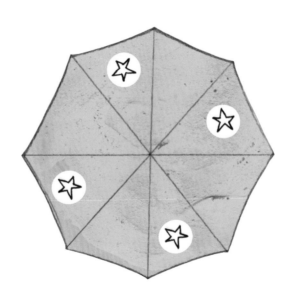

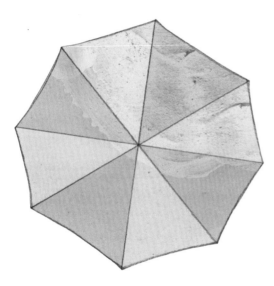
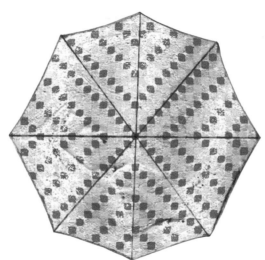

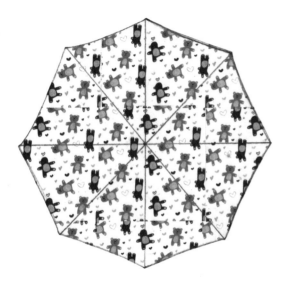

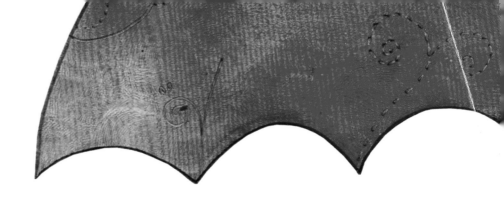

The Thingamabob

Il Sung Na

Alfred A. Knopf · New York

One day,
he found the
thingamabob.

He had no idea
what the thingamabob was
or where it came from.

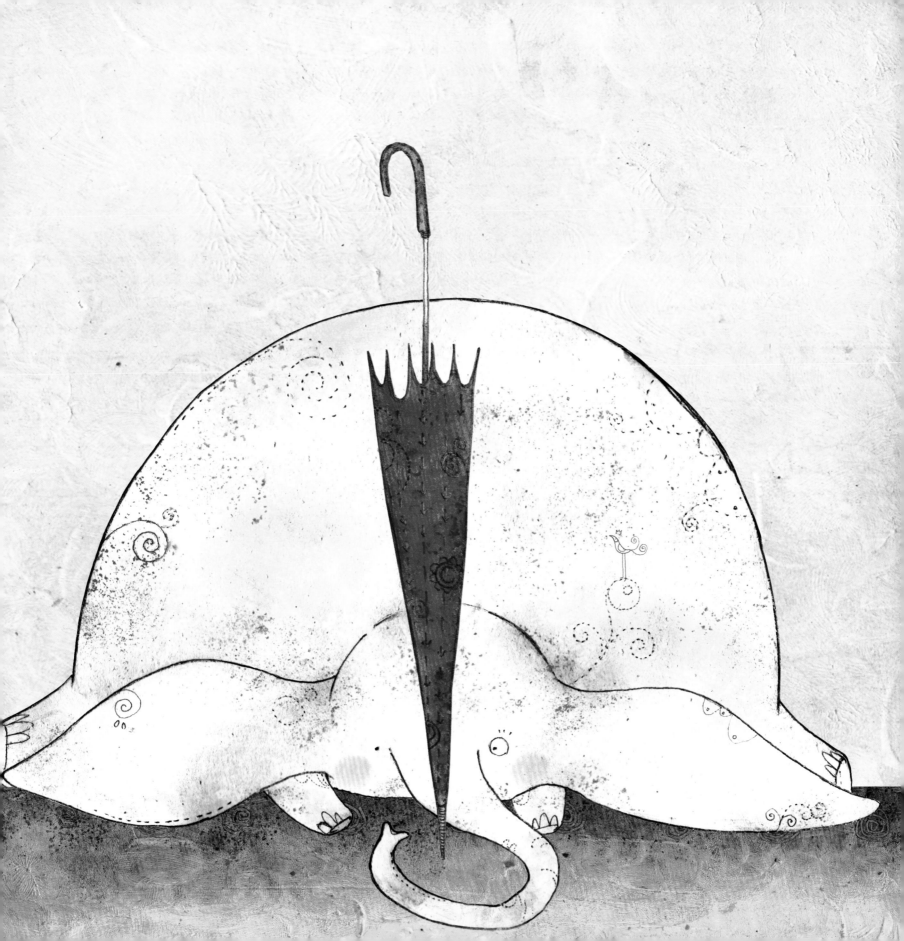

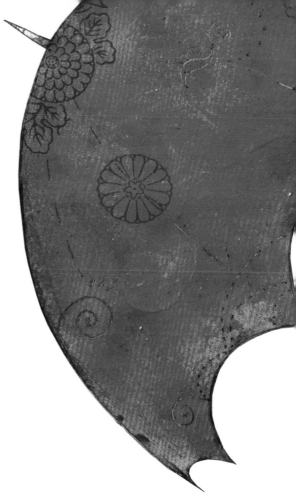

Sometimes,
it didn't do anything at all.

Sometimes,
it gave him a surprise!

He asked his friends...

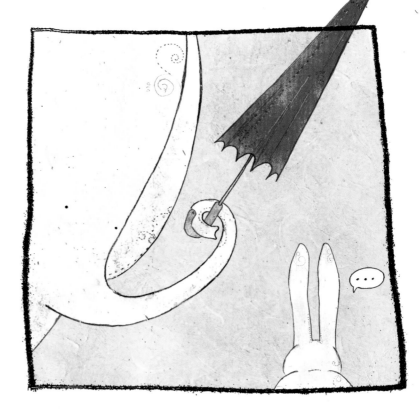

...but they did not
seem to know.

He thought...
Maybe I can fly with it?

Maybe not.

Maybe I can sail in it?

Maybe not.

Maybe I can hide
behind it?

Maybe not.

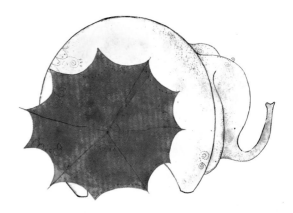

"What are you, then?!"
he cried.

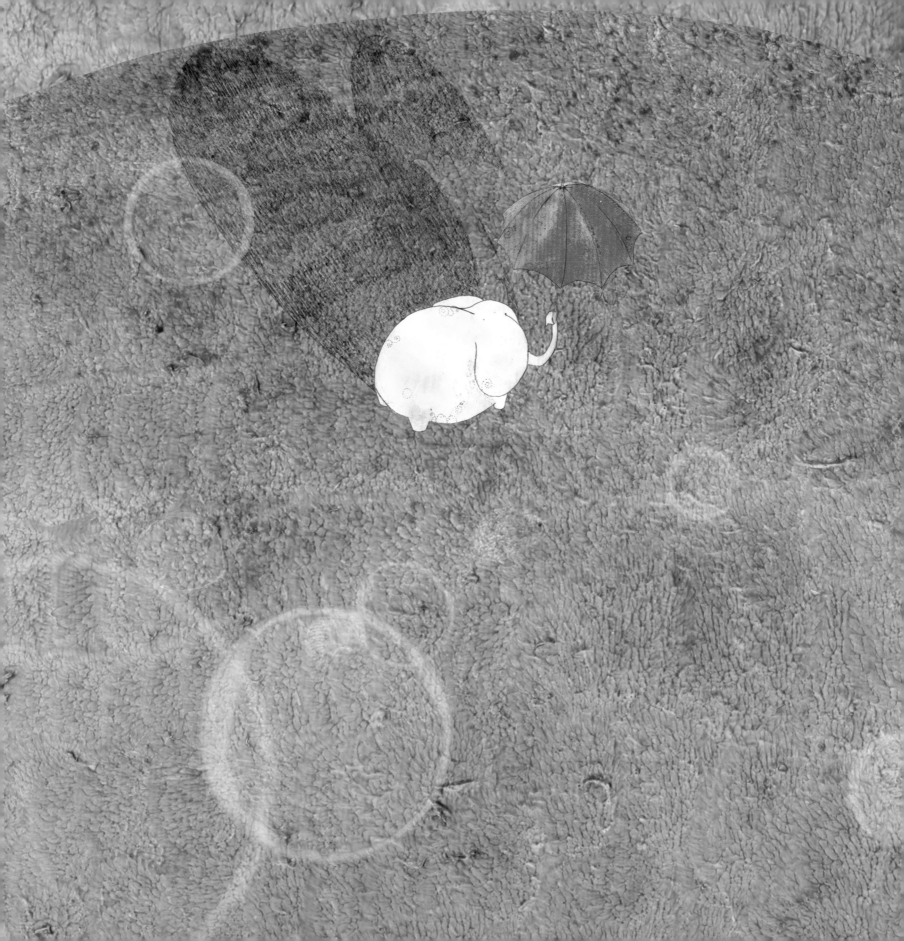

Then
big
drops
of rain
started
to fall.

He did
not want
to get wet.

He did not need
to get wet!

And neither did his friends.

For my nephew Rueben

THIS IS A BORZOI BOOK PUBLISHED BY ALFRED A. KNOPF

Copyright © 2008 by Il Sung Na

Visit us on the Web! www.randomhouse.com/kids

Educators and librarians, for a variety of teaching tools, visit us at
www.randomhouse.com/teachers

Library of Congress Cataloging-in-Publication Data
Na, Il Sung.
The thingamabob / Il Sung Na. — 1st American ed.
    p.   cm.
"Originally published in slightly different form in great Britain by Meadowside Children's Books, London, in 2008"—Copr. p.
Summary: An elephant finds a "thingamabob" and experiments until he discovers what to do with it.
ISBN 978-0-375-86106-2 (trade) — ISBN 978-0-375-96106-9 (lib. bdg.)
[1. Elephants—Fiction. 2. Umbrellas—Fiction.] I. Title.
PZ7.N1244Th 2010
[E]—dc22
2009003120

The illustrations in this book were created by combining handmade painterly textures
with digitally generated layers, which were then compiled in Adobe Photoshop.

MANUFACTURED IN CHINA
March 2010
10 9 8 7 6 5 4 3 2 1

First American Edition

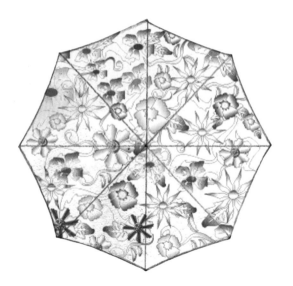
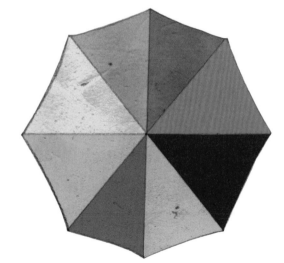
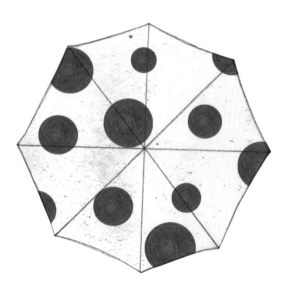
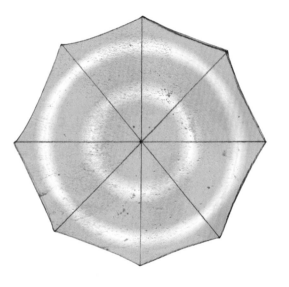

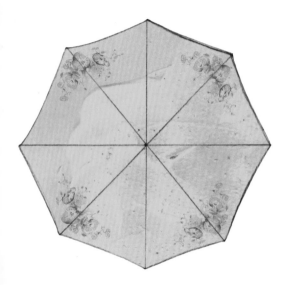

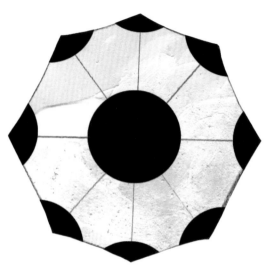